A Note to Parents and Caregivers:

Read-it! Readers are for children who are just starting on the amazing road to reading. These beautiful books support both the acquisition of reading skills and the love of books.

 The PURPLE LEVEL presents basic topics and objects using high frequency words and simple language patterns.

 The RED LEVEL presents familiar topics using common words and repeating sentence patterns.

 The BLUE LEVEL presents new ideas using a larger vocabulary and varied sentence structure.

 The YELLOW LEVEL presents more challenging ideas, a broad vocabulary, and wide variety in sentence structure.

 The GREEN LEVEL presents more complex ideas, an extended vocabulary range, and expanded language structures.

 The ORANGE LEVEL presents a wide range of ideas and concepts using challenging vocabulary and complex language structures.

When sharing a book with your child, read in short stretches, pausing often to talk about the pictures. Have your child turn the pages and point to the pictures and familiar words. And be sure to reread favorite stories or parts of stories.

There is no right or wrong way to share books with children. Find time to read with your child, and pass on the legacy of literacy.

Adria F. Klein, Ph.D.
Professor Emeritus
California State University
San Bernardino, California

Editor: Nick Healy
Designer: Nathan Gassman
Page Production: Lori Bye
Creative Director: Keith Griffin
Editorial Director: Carol Jones
The illustrations in this book were created with watercolor.

Picture Window Books
5115 Excelsior Boulevard
Suite 232
Minneapolis, MN 55416
877-845-8392
www.picturewindowbooks.com

Printed in the United States of America.

Library of Congress Cataloging-in-Publication Data
Dougherty, Terri.
The flying fish / by Terri Dougherty ; illustrated by Kristy Visser.
p. cm. — (Read-it! readers)
Summary: When Rachel goes fishing with her grandfather, she wonders if she will
ever catch anything.
ISBN-13: 978-1-4048-2410-2 (hardcover)
ISBN-10: 1-4048-2410-3 (hardcover)
[1. Fishing—Fiction. 2. Grandfathers—Fiction. 3. Asian Americans—Fiction.]
I. Visser, Kristy, 1984- , ill. II. Title. III. Series.
PZ7.D74436Fly 2006
[E]—dc22   2006003579

The Flying Fish

by Terri Dougherty
illustrated by Kristy Visser

Special thanks to our advisers for their expertise:

Adria F. Klein, Ph.D.
Professor Emeritus, California State University
San Bernardino, California

Susan Kesselring, M.A.
Literacy Educator
Rosemount–Apple Valley–Eagan (Minnesota) School District

PICTURE WINDOW BOOKS
Minneapolis, Minnesota

Rachel and Grandpa were ready to fish. Rachel asked, "Will we catch some fish today?"

"I hope so," Grandpa said.

Rachel sat under a tree by the pond. Her line wiggled. Her pole jiggled. The bobber dipped under the water.

"I caught a fish!" she yelled.

She reeled in the line and pulled the fish out of the water. She swung it toward the net. The fish flopped off the hook. It landed in the pond.

"Will I catch another fish today?" Rachel asked.

Grandpa said, "I hope you catch another fish today."

Rachel stood near the shore. Soon, her line wiggled. Her pole jiggled. The bobber dropped under the water.

Rachel tried to reel in the line. She tugged and pulled. She brought the hook out of the water.

There was something long and green on the end. It was a weed.

"Will I ever catch another fish?"
Rachel asked.

"I'm sure you will catch another
fish," Grandpa said.

Rachel leaned against the tree. Before long, her line wiggled. Her pole jiggled. The bobber dove under the water.

Rachel jerked the pole. She reeled in the line.

She pulled hard and yanked the fish out of
the water.

The fish flew over Rachel's head. The line wrapped around a branch above the water. The fish dangled over the pond.

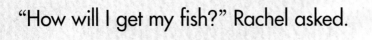
"How will I get my fish?" Rachel asked.

Grandpa looked at the fish hanging from the branch. A man in a boat rowed by.

"Can you please get my fish?" Rachel asked.

The man paddled toward the fish. He tugged the fish off the hook and brought it to shore.

Rachel looked at the fish. It flipped and flopped.

The fish tried hard to get back into the water.

"Do you want your fish?" the man asked.

Rachel took the fish and threw it into the pond.

"This fish can go back into the water today,"
Rachel said. "I'll catch another fish tomorrow."

More *Read-it!* Readers

Bright pictures and fun stories help you practice your reading skills. Look for more books at your level.

Bamboo at the Beach 1-4048-1035-8

The Best Lunch 1-4048-1578-3

Car Shopping 1-4048-2406-5

Clinks the Robot 1-4048-1579-1

Flynn Flies High 1-4048-0563-X

Freddie's Fears 1-4048-0056-5

Loop, Swoop, and Pull! 1-4048-1611-9

Marvin, the Blue Pig 1-4048-0564-8

Megan Has to Move 1-4048-1613-5

Moo! 1-4048-0643-1

My Favorite Monster 1-4048-1029-3

Pippin's Big Jump 1-4048-0555-9

Pony Party 1-4048-1612-7

Rudy Helps Out 1-4048-2420-0

The Snow Dance 1-4048-2421-9

Sounds Like Fun 1-4048-0649-0

The Ticket 1-4048-2423-5

Tired of Waiting 1-4048-0650-4

Whose Birthday Is It? 1-4048-0554-0

Looking for a specific title or level? A complete list of *Read-it!* Readers is available on our Web site:

www.picturewindowbooks.com